This page intentionally left blank

1.God's own Country

The highlands to the north of Kerala were once draped in dense forest. The thick tropical forest was home to a rich diversity of animal life. There were marauding, majestic elephant herds. Lurking in the dark recesses of the forest were a contagion of leopards and the occasional regal tiger. The big cats performed the critical function of culling exuberant herds of deer to ecologically appropriate balances. A pandemonium of primates competed with a cacophony of colorful birds for primacy beneath the leafy cascades of tropical trees.

The English had set up a few tea plantations and experimented with rubber cultivation. There were very few human settlements. Very few men ventured into these areas. A few intrepid plantation owners, cleared hill sides forests for cultivation. They built rest houses for themselves and barracks for the estate workers. The estates were pockets of civilization. Children's schools and shops were created.

There were settlers in the forest too. They came from princely states of Travancore and Cochin. There were some from Malabar. Many of them had run away to the hills to escape the obscurity of social ostracization or the wrath of the ruling disposition. There were some who had opted to get away from the mainstream of Travancore to escape pecuniary penury. An adventurous few who were out to seek their fortune or to escape the long arm of conventional justice completed the mix.

These settlements often proliferated to create temporary townships. Provisions were procured from the Kottayam market. Bullock carts and later jeeps were the vehicles for transport of people and for replenishment of stocks. Goods transported from the town ranged from food grains and agricultural tools to fabrics and jewelry. On the return leg they carted bananas, jackfruit and forest produce to the market. There were a few tribal villages inside the jungle. The tribals depended on settlers for trinkets and for information. They brought for barter, animal skins and herbs. Tribal villages were far apart and few in number. They hunted with bow and arrow and mainly lived off the forest. The life of a tribal in the jungle fraught with peril.

In settlements, everyone minded his or her business. Life here was too rigorous for gossip and too intense to condone casual socializing. Survival depended on mutual trust. Strong bonds ensured equitably shared burdens. Settlers banded together to tackle wild animal intrusions and to tackle other common concerns. Contrary to expectations, the lack of law enforcement did not beget lawlessness. Many of the settlers had violent pasts. They were however men of honor. Natural justice and fairness prevailed. Joys and sorrows were shared.

Everyone was equal here. Yet, in every society there are legends. Raghavan was one of them. To the police and the government administrators, Raghavan Velu was a brigand or a bandit. To settlers and to the tribals, Raghavan was a demi-god. Settlers and those who resided in the villages below, revered him. The village folk spoke of him as the 'Anai-thalavan', or 'the king of the elephants. It was village lore that Raghavan never forgot a favor or forgave an insult.

2.Romance and Elopement:

The story and the legend of Raghavan was common knowledge. Raghavan was an educated man. Shumbani was an untouchable. She was from a caste considered inferior and menial by traditional Hindu society. Abandoned as an orphan, by her teenage mother, she had been educated by the British Regent's wife. Raghavan met Shumbani at the Ravi Varma academy of ayurvedic medicine and traditional art. This academy had been established by the royal family of Travancore to nurture and to preserve traditional Kerala art forms. It was later run by the British. Shumbani worked in this gallery as a curate. Raghavan, fondly called Raghu by his associates was an art aficionado. He also dabbled in ayurvedic medicines and in Kalarippayattu.

Raghavan's father was the commander of the imperial guard of the Travancore emperor. He was a scion of the Nair Community. Nairs are the warrior class in the Kerala royal Pantheon. When Raghavan met Shumbani, an untouchable, and fell in love with her, he was cocking a snoot at Kerala customs and his heritage. He incurred the wrath of his clan.

The caste system had been legally banished by the British. Social barriers however, were as rigid as ever. Transgressors were ostracized and often eliminated. A bunch of radical vigilantes had attempted to reclaim the clan's honor with Raghu's blood. Raghavan was not easy to kill. His mastery of the martial art of Kalarippayattu had saved his life. He and Shumbani escaped from Travancore in the dead of the night. and made their way to the high ranges. Here men and women were governed and gauged by their worth and not their lineage.

3. A Home in the Forest:

There were jeep tracks leading through the forest to the tea estates. It was by the side of such a track, at the edge of the forest, that Raghavan and Shumbani made their home. A few more huts sprang up soon after. They soon had a township of sorts. This was forest land belonging to no one, The government encouraged settlement in these areas. The rule was that the holdings could be registered with the district authority at Kottayam. There was a registration fee which helped buff up the treasury.

Settlers planted tapioca and grew vegetables. The men hunted deer and squirrels. These animal skins could be traded at the nearest town for rice, lentils and clothes. They got kitchen utensils, axes, spades, kerosene for their lamps and various other things that the forest could not provide from the market in town. Life was wholesome. The land was fertile. The forest was rich in Flora, Fauna and Fruit.

Raghavan got the settlers organized. They set up a local panchayat. They went to the government office and had all the township holdings of land registered. The settlers now owned the land they farmed. As the township grew, a couple of shops sprouted. Shop owners organized the logistics of procurement and provisioning. There was no medical care. Raghu was the resident doctor. With his knowledge of ayurveda and his reserve of common sense he could decide what ailments and injuries he could manage and what cases needed transfer to the hospital at Kottayam.

Years went by. The township was relatively prosperous. Families flourished. Children grew up. Shumbani set up a school for the children of the settlement. The school house was an improvised shed on their property. She was the sole teacher. She taught children and the ladies to read and to write. She taught the children mathematics and the sciences. As the township grew, her work increased. The local shop would procure study material for her from a bookstall at Kottayam. Shumbani was busy from dawn to dusk.

Shumbani wanted to get her school recognized. This would help her students to get jobs in town or to pursue higher education at the colleges in Madras. To qualify as a school, she would need at least one more teacher. She soon got help. A young couple who had married against their parent's express orders escaped retribution and sought sanctuary in the settlement. They hitched a ride in an estate jeep. In the Jeep, during the ride, they confided in the Jeep driver, soliciting his guidance on settling down to a new life of peace and fulfillment in the hills. The jeep driver knew of Raghu and Shumbani. They had a reputation for unequivocal compassion backed by unrivalled courage. The driver dropped the distraught couple at their door.

Shumbani and Raghu received them and

gave them food. They housed them in the school shed. Dilip and Sarita were grateful. The shed evolved into night house for them. In the morning, Dilip would go with Raghu into the fields and the Forest. Sarita would help Shumbani with the classes. Sarita was good at music. They procured a second-hand harmonica through the local shop. Sarita taught the children music. Raghavan and Shumbani had two sons. They attended school in the morning, but in the evenings, they would accompany their father on some short hunting expeditions.

4.A Sinister visit and horrendous attack:

One afternoon, a police posse paid a visit to the hamlet. With the policemen was a wealthy looking man with a score of gold rings on his fingers. Some of the men in the settlement recognized him. They had seen his photograph in the newspapers. He was a state minister. He was notorious for corruption and graft. It was rumored that he had master minded and executed many land grabs. He acted on behalf of wealthy conglomerates and at the behest of ambitious relatives. The group sauntered around the settlement and left without speaking to anyone. Raghavan called a meeting of the panchayat. They were all worried about the minister's visit, but the land had been registered in their names. The law was on their side.

A week had passed since the mysterious visit and Raghavan had gone hunting alone in the forest. Today, the trail of deer led him across the range of hills to a valley many miles away. A true hunter, he would never kill the doe or the young deer, only the magnificent stags, the swiftest and meatiest of the pack. The rumble of vehicles on the estate road faded away as he sprinted through the forest, with his poised spear. The running stag had outsmarted many a hunter and left many a leopard hungry and frustrated.

Shumbani and Sarita were conducting class when the trucks and jeeps rolled up. Leaving Sarita to continue with the class, she had gone to investigate. What she saw was petrifying. Hooded goons were leaping off the trucks and invading the settlement. Some carried lighted torches and some had swords. She watched aghast as women were being dragged behind bushes and men in the settlement were beaten into submission. She rushed to the school hall screaming- 'Run-run". Children scrambled out of the hall and escaped into the forest. She ran into the forest with them to help them to hide.

There was a small grassy plain surrounded by a ring of trees. She sprinted across the field helping the children along. There was a small cave in the hillside. She hid them there and camouflaged the cave mouth with vegetation. She admonished some crying children, goading them into silence. She looked behind in consternation. Where was Sarita?

She ran back to the school hall. Most of the houses including hers were on fire. There was no way to salvage anything from the roaring flames. The school hall was not burning. There seemed to be no one inside. Suddenly she heard a whimper from a corner. A drunken goon was rising to his feet. On the floor, huddled up and gathering her torn clothes around herself, Sarita was whimpering. Something snapped inside Sumathi. Roaring in rage, she picked up sharp iron rod and charged at Sumathi's tormentor. She did not see another goon stepping out of the shadows behind her. He brought his lathi crashing down on Shumbani's head. Shumbani crumbled to the ground. As the consciousness ebbed out of her Neurons, she heard the first goon say with a leer. "You should not have killed her. We could have used her first".

5. The Hunter becomes Prey:

Raghu was deep inside the forest, in the valley across the mountain range. The stag was drained. The hunter on his trail was legendary. The animal was soon aware that this could be his last run. He felt no fear. Death would come when it would come. He would give life his all. He would make the hunter earn his trophy. There was glory and honor in falling to a worthy opponent. Raghu's reserves were running low. Finally, he out-maneuvered the stag, skirting a patch of thick forest. His spear impaled the magnificent creature's torso. The animal stopped in its tracks. The wizened head with its magnificent crown of antlers turned to look at Raghu as he emerged from behind the trees. Man, and animal looked at each other with mutual respect. The stag seemed to acknowledge a master. Raghu looked back at the magnificent animal. He expected the animal to fall down and die. Incredibly and against all odds, the animal started running again. Ahead was a steep cliff. If it crested the cliff, it would fall dead into the flooded river below. Raghu would not be denied his prize. He flung himself in a tackle at the stag's neck and wrestled him to the ground. The animal's eyes rolled up as life fizzed out through his punctured chest. The battle was over.

Raghu turned back, triumphant yet strangely subdued. The death of an opponent worthy of respect offers a moment of reflection. It is then that we are intensely aware of our own vulnerability. As he crested the mountain on his return, the dead stag across his broad shoulders, he saw smoke rising from his township. Dropping the dead animal, he ran to a clearing from where he could see the settlement better. There was a large group of people milling around. Most structures had been incinerated to cinder. A few remaining houses of the settlement houses were on fire.

A convoy of trucks parked on the jeep

track were being filled up with people. Raghavan started sprinting down to the settlement, but he was quite a distance away and the last of the trucks had left before he could reach. The settlement, including his house had been razed to the ground. There was a board that had been put up by the raiders, which read, "Honest Lumber Company" and below that, in smaller letters, "trespassers will be prosecuted".

Ravi, one of his neighbors was hiding in the bushes behind the settlement. He described the attack by the minister's men. The group of goons, some of them policemen in mufti, had rolled up in five trucks and a police van. They had bundled the men into the police van and then had looted the houses before setting them ablaze. Shumbani had resisted and one of the men had hit her on the head with a lathi. The goons and the minister left.

A jeep and a pick-up truck had come from the estate soon after. The estate manager had seen the fire and sent his team to investigate. Shumbani had been taken to the Medical College at Kottayam in an unconscious state. Her two sons went with her. They were too young to comprehend what had happened. The fire and violence they witnessed seemed part of a nightmare. Other survivors were bundled into the pickup truck which would take them to the estate. They could then be transported across the border to Madras. The goons would harm them if they were to come down to Kottayam. They would be averse to having witnesses to the carnage they had committed.

6. Shumbani undergoes Brain Surgery:

There were no vehicles to take Raghu to town. The estate jeep would be available only after a couple of days. The jeep would go back to the estate and then return on the town run a day later. Raghu had a brain wave. There was a tribal village deep in the forest, a few kilometers away. He was friendly with the tribal chief and had once rescued the chief's son from the coils of a giant python. During his last visit to the village, the chief had showed him a new acquisition. A visiting British anthropologist had gifted the chief a bicycle. None of the Tribals could ride a cycle. Raghu had tried to teach them how to ride the cycle. As far as he knew, the cycle was still a decorative piece in the chief's hut.

Raghavan ran through the forest to the tribal village. The tribals knew that things were amiss at the settlement. They had seen the fire and smoke and heard the rumble of trucks. They stayed out of trouble by turning a blind eye on government excesses and police atrocities. Raghu told them what he wanted. The chief immediately rolled the bicycle out of his hut for Raghu. Thanking the chief, Raghu started out down the dirt track and road. He reached town in a couple of hours.

The gates of the hospital had been closed for the night. There was an irate sentry at the gate adept at turning back all intruders. Raghu's personality was persuasive. The sentry unlocked the door to let him in and guided him to the operation theatre. Shumabani's surgery was over. She had been shifted to the intensive care unit which had been recently inaugurated by the erstwhile Maharaja. The royal family had sponsored the construction. The recently elected state government had taken credit. Politicians were yet to master the art of vote getting photo ops.

Shumbani's mother, now worked as an assistant to the missionary school headmistress near Kottayam. She had heard of the attack and was already there, at the hospital. Raghu's two sons were being consoled by their grandmother. Raghavan remained by his wife's bed as she recovered slowly. Her right side was weak and she had difficulty in speaking, but she survived. She could not remember what happened at the settlement. It was all too well. There were people observing her. If her memories had returned, they would have ensured her perpetual silence.

Shumbani had lost some of her memories. She could not remember her relationship with Raghu. She would sob and say that her husband had been killed by an elephant. Her conviction was so strong that the children were brainwashed. They were soon convinced that Raghu was their uncle.

7. Starting a New Life:

Raghavan wondered how he would earn a livelihood. His skills in the forest were wasted in the evolving, increasingly chaotic concrete jungle of Kottayam town. Raghu was realistic and pragmatic. It was best to close the chapter on the massacre at the forest township for the sake of his family. Shumbani would not be able to live in a forest settlement anymore.

Her mother confided their problems to the school headmistress. The school needed an estate manager. Raghavan was offered the appointment. The arrangement suited everyone. Under Raghu's deft carousal, the estate flourished. The estate managers house was an idyllic cottage beside a bubbly stream. The children enjoyed the scenic gardens and the sublime peace. Shumbani was making a rapid recovery. She was soon able to care for herself. Her memories and manners were restored. Her skills were intact and her intellect uninhibited. Her memory and learning were mostly retained, barring the fortuitous blank period around the assault.

Raghavan and his family settled in the mission campus near Kottayam. Raghu could do the work of ten men and still look for more. The estate flourished. His sons attended the school. Their memories of the assault at the old settlement faded amidst the joys of childhood and the symphony of schooling. As Shumbani recovered she was made the school librarian. She was normal to all appearances and was being restored to her former facile ebullience.

Few noticed the simmering tensions beneath Raghu's bland devotion to garden and estate maintenance. A few birds in the estate had their nightly séance interrupted by crisply scintillating Kalari displays at midnight. Raghu was in training. Birds enthralled at his performance would chatter their indecipherable tales of the great warrior who masqueraded as a gardener during the day. A wise old owl whispered to her owlets, "All hell is going to break loose. Thank God I am not a politician".

8. Justice and Revenge:

Two years went by. The minister who had robbed them of their home, levelihood and honor was now the chief minister. Elections were only a few months away. Raghu stayed away from politics. He had never voted and showed no inclination to get himself registered in the electoral rolls. The school headmistress commented to her friends, "Raghu is such a sweet, soft and simple soul. All he cares about is his garden".

One day Raghavan had gone to the town to buy an axe for chopping firewood. He was on his way back, when he found the road blocked. A political meeting was in progress and the chief minister was addressing a mammoth rally. Raghu vaulted over the fence and stepped closer to listen.

The politician was a charismatic orator. Despite his animosity, Raghavan was impressed by the magnetism he exerted over the crowd. It was jarring and difficult to reconcile his erudite oration with his criminal and violent antecedents. Many in the crowd were aware that this benevolent leader had made his fortune and his career through murder and Dacoity. They were also aware that he was continuing to loot the people of the state. In closed rooms and in alcohol enabled political discussions at the Ravi Verma Club, he was derisively described at Minister 50%. That was his share in land grabs, illicit logging and smuggling operations. Yet caste and political considerations and business compulsions ensured him wide and election winning support. The intelligentsia of the state wondered where he slashed all his loot.

"I have dedicated my life to the service of the people of this state", the honorable chief minister said. "Till every Keralite has a roof over his head, I shall not rest", he concluded. The crowd loved the clichés and the applause was deafening. The speech was over. Now it was question time. Raghavan inched forward to listen. There was a reporter with allegiance to a rival group who was bent upon asking difficult questions. "There were some allegations about the role you played in a land grab in the high ranges a couple of years ago" the reporter paused as the crowd heckled him. A few lathi wielding policemen moved menacingly towards him. "There was a prostitution racket in the hills, which I stopped", replied the minister. "I can understand your frustration. You may have been a patron. But I will not let this glorious state to be sullied by decadence.

The crowd roared its approval. Something snapped inside Raghavan's brain. With a roar, he somersaulted on to the podium, his axe in his hand. With one swipe of his woodcutters axe he chopped off the minister's head, holding it up for all to see, as the man's body crumbled to the ground, still clutching the microphone in a lifeless hand. There was a high boundary wall behind the stage. As the policemen and the crowd froze in shock, Raghu swung himself over the fifteen-foot wall to escape seemingly into thin air. The assailant's identity would remain a mystery forever. There were allegations of an international conspiracy and of a 'red hand'.

9. Raghu returns to the Forest:

Raghavan made his way to the forest. He retrieved the bicycle the tribal chief had lent him. If he remained in town, it was possible that someone would recognize him. He scribbled a note to Shumbani. "A friend has asked for my help to rescue a child lost in the woods. I will come when my work is finished. Look after the boys". Shumbani heard of the grisly assassination. She wished Raghu was around to tell her the details.

Iconic investigative agencies worked overtime to decipher the enigma behind the state leader's assassination. The press claimed to have traced and tracked the killers. They had evidence to show that the assassination team was trained in a neighboring hostile country. The route the killers took was diligently traced. The United Nations was alerted to issue a red corner alert for a terror lynchpin who had taken refuge in the Middle East. The motive behind the murder was speculated. The minister had enemies. He had incurred the ire of the political class with his frugal lifestyle and refusal to indulge in political handouts. A statue of the honest politician was unveiled in the city. There was much mourning.

The investigative journalism was much acclaimed and two journalists felicitated for their pioneering work. The police were happy. The local police force was not equipped to repel an organized terror attack funded in petro-dollars. They were exonerated. Special funds were allotted to the police for state-of-the-art weaponry. A speed boat was procured for them to intercept suspicious vessels along the Kerala coast line. A special hazard duty allowance would be sanctioned to members of the force.

Shumbani's mother and the missionaries had no inkling of Raghu's role in the chief minister's assassination. They wished he were around. With terrorists roaming around town, an additional male would be an asset. Even a docile and innocuous man like Raghu, on the property would have be an additional peg of security. They believed that the lure of the forest had become too strong for him to resist. The missionary's wife was compassionate. "Raghu had been working too hard", she surmised. He must have had a burn out. News of the terror attack in town would have scared him. He would be back once he restored his confidence in himself".

Raghu cycled up through the hill roads. The number of trucks plying these roads had increased exponentially. Raghu watched the scenery as he pedaled up the deserted roads.

The high ranges where Raghavan had built his house were transformed. The hill had been denuded of its forest cover. The 'Honest Timber Township' was a mini city with bars and night clubs. A dozen lumber trucks were in the clearing, loaded with huge logs. Pretending to be a lumberman looking for work, Raghavan befriended one of the security officers of the town. That night over bottles of toddy and plates of fried 'chemmeen', he gathered intelligence.

The lumber company was owned by a business magnate who had an iron grip over Kerala politics. The chief minister had been his man. With the minister's tragic demise, another stooge was already being groomed for his chair. Half the proceeds of the timber business went to the cops and the political patrons. The initial investment was negligible. Trees were being cut from forest land. There was still big money for all concerned.

Raghavan did not want to stay in the township. He had decided to complete his journey of revenge. The fewer people he met, the better. There was still dense forest on the neighboring hills. Raghu cycled to the forest. He tracked the tribal settlement easily. The chief was happy to see him. Raghu returned him his ole bicycle. He also gifted him a Rolex watch. The missionary's wife had gifted him this expensive watch as a token of appreciation for his work. Raghavan walked deep into the forest till he found a secluded spot surrounded by trees. There was a stream running close by. Raghavan set up camp.

There was excited chatter amongst the monkeys. A King Cobra came to investigate. Raghu was sitting propped up against a tree. The cobra raised his head and spread his hood. He glared at Raghu who glared right back at him. Slowly the cobra lowered his head. He had been sent by the forest spirits to confirm that the monkeys were right. This was the great hunter, Raghu. The wind whispered through the trees. The man god is back. The forest will be saved.

10. Saving the Forest:

In the wee hours of the morning Raghavan struck. The night clubs had closed and the hostesses had been sent back to their hotel in town. Lights were dimmed. There were two security men on duty at the township. They had just consumed a fair bit of toddy and were nodding off. The sleepy security detail on duty posed no problems for him. Hard knocks to head in quick succession rendered them blithely unaware of the proceedings. Slinging the security men, one over each shoulder he carried them across the lorry bay before dumping them in the forest. Returning to the parked trucks he prized their fuel tanks open, one by one. Petrol seeped into wet mud creating a combustible mix. Casually, he flicked a lighted match stick into the grime before stepping back.

The burning lumber trucks set up a rich

blaze which colored the forest skies crimson. Drivers tumbled out of the huts where they were resting. There was little they could do. The inferno was too intense. Fortunately, the fire did not extend to the hutments. The trucks were charred to cindered skeletons. The fire team and a police posse were sent for damage control from Kottayam town. The charred skeletons of a dozen trucks gave one the impression that a bomb had gone off in the vicinity.

The police started their investigations. The drivers had no idea how the fire started. Garbled stories of the security detail mentioned a bunch of supermen who descended on them like biblical avenging angels. The security men claimed to have fought them off initially, but had been overwhelmed by the sheer savagery of the troupe. Their stated assessment of the number of attackers varied from 5 to 15.

The leader of the avenging troupe was described as a 7-foot-tall man with long flowing hair. The newspapers had a field day. There were myriad hypotheses. It was postulated that the troupe was of Greek descent. A bunch of soldiers from Alexander's army had established a settlement in the forests of North Kerala. The legend was that the goddess of the forest entrusted the safety of the forest to these warriors. They guarded the forest and the forest sustained them.

A legend was born. The political patrons and business magnates who had financed the logging venture were furious. Myth and fantasy would keep the common man entertained and occupied. Only a resumption of illicit logging would sustain affluence and with it, influence. A police posse was detailed to track down this menace.

The election results were out. A new leader had taken over the reins of chief minister-ship. With the opportunism of a true politician, the new chief minister blamed all the deforestation on this brigand. The police filed a report on the myriad gangs who had sought refuge and executed criminal activities from the forests of North Kerala. There were Naxalites convicts and drug dealers. Raghu had encountered these groups during his hunting forays into the forest when he stayed in the forest township. He had given them wide berth. In turn the gangs left the settlers alone.

News snippets kept the Kerala forests in the spotlight. There were concerns from the west over illicit drugs being routed through India to markets in Europe and the USA. Recent intelligence inputs had suggested a drug route through the Kerala forests. There was strong evidence that a drug refinery and purification unit was being set up in the forests. Central and state governments vehemently denied allegations that the drug chain was routed through Kerala.

Political payoffs and patronage by the

drug cartel were a dirty secret that most people were aware of. There was a lot of money in drugs. The drug cartel was sponsored by a south American government. A local Mafia chief ran the operations. Drug money kept the economy afloat sponsored don. Illicit drug money Financed government enterprise and kept the economy afloat.

The drug cartel deployed a private army of over a hundred men. These men, maintained discipline down the chain. They supervised the opium harvest, guarded drug mules or drug carriers and protected the factories where opium was distilled for heroin and synthetic drugs were made. Kerala operations were still at an early stage.

A rubber factory at the edge of the forest which operated under the aegis of the state Rubber Board was being modified to distill and purify opium to morphine. Another factory in Europe would distill heroin from morphine. The last thing any government would want to have drug factories exposed in their territory. The government had clout over the environmental lobby. They could stymie intrusions and explorations into the forest by declaring protected eco-sensitive zones. With Raghu hiding in the forests, the government was averse to large scale military operations in the forest. The illicit drug route needed to be rerouted and all traces of drug purification wiped clean before any major operation was launched. This brought Raghu and the forest some respite.

Raghavan was like a vengeful angel. The forest had been his home for many a year and the first foolhardy group of local policemen who tried to chase him found themselves impaled on spikes in an elephant pit. Another troupe had a bee hive fall upon them. Raghu had no enmity with the foot policemen. He minimized damage while maximizing deterrence. In the floundering police operations against Raghu no one died.

The injuries and the embarrassment however were profound.

The police party changed their strategy. There was pressure on them to facilitate revival of logging. They switched tack. A fair-sized police posse provided protection to the settlement. Police jeeps would be deployed to escort convoys of lumbering trucks. The plans looked good on paper. Raghavan had other ideas. The road to Kottayam was through the forested hills where Raghavan could strike with impunity. Landslides were engineered and too many of the loaded trucks landed at the bottom of the gorge. The contractors backed off. They could find no one to pay off for protection. The costs kept rising. Lumbering operations had been effectively stymied. The police claimed many arrests from the brigand's band, detaining innocent villagers and immigrant laborers from the nearby states.

11. A strategic Retreat:

The contractor was livid. Politicians were being starved of their regular incomes. The chief minister approached the central government. This uproar was inevitable. One Brigand had stymied the political machinery. This was anarchy at its worst. The angst permeated down from the middle levels of the system. The real powers who conducted the puppet show were unfazed. The drug route had been redrawn. An African military coup had brought in a sympathetic general with liberal values. The factory in the Kerala Forest had started making rubber flipflops and contraceptive sheaths again.

A coordinated search by police commando and army units experienced in jungle warfare was launched. Raghavan slipped out of the hills and into the neighboring state of Tamilnadu. He opened a roadside restaurant there which soon had a roaring business. Police and the army combed the jungles for the Brigand. Raghavan's café did brisk business providing tea and snacks to security personnel on this mission. The security search patrols confined their intrusions to safe zones during the day. The only confrontations they encountered were from abusive and rancorous monkeys.

The public wanted spicy updates. The newspapers provided that. The papers were full of stories about the continuing battle in the hills. Radio broadcasts tracked the battle zones and bet on outcomes. Many police and army personnel were decorated for their courage. Raghavan's tea stall flourished. The popularity rating of the political party in power reached new heights the day they announced that the brigand had been killed in an encounter.

Raghavan chuckled as he read the headlines. He empathized with the innocent who had been sacrificed in his place. Now it was safe for him to contact his family and to return to Kottayam. He made inquiries regarding his family from truck driver from Kottayam. The trucker knew of the mission school where Shumbani worked. She apparently had recovered. She was teaching in school. Her intellect was intact. She had retained her memories from childhood. Her recent memory and cognition were intact. Interestingly, there was a decade long gap in her memory archives from her school days to her recovery at the mission. Raghu sent a letter through the trucker to be given to Shumbani.

12. Raghu returns to Kottayam:

The security forces were being withdrawn in phases. The Tea stall would soon be redundant and revenues would nosedive. Raghu was looking for someone to sell or hand over his Tea Shop to. He soon found a buyer. A gulf-based businessman who owned a rubber factory in the forest region was looking for a hotel. He would buy Raghu's tea-stall and construct a rest house there. This hotel which would serve as a base camp for employees and for visitors.

Raghu sold the tea stall. He had sent a message through the Trucker that he would be returning to Kottayam. He wondered if she would remember him. When he returned to Kottayam Shumbani and their sons were ecstatic. They had assumed that he had been killed in the forest by the Forest Brigand who was in the news. They quizzed him regarding his prolonged absence from the scene. Raghu averred that he was afraid the authorities would accuse him of the chief minister's murder. He had sought refuge in Tamil Nadu and had run a Tea Shop there.

Shumbani did not remember Raghu as a spouse. She seemed to believe that Raghu was her brother. She claimed that her husband had been killed by a temple elephant during a festival. Someone set off crackers during a temple procession and the elephant had run amok. Her husband had stepped out in its path to stop him. The elephant had been brought back in control. However, in a fit of anguished rage, the tusker had punctured her husband's chest. He had died instantly. It was all sheer confabulation. Yet, Raghu could trace the correlation. He had been the Anaithalavan or king of the elephants to the residents of the northern settlements and townships.

Raghu's sons remembered him. They, however seemed to believe their mother's version of who he was. They called him uncle. Raghu was appalled. He went to Shumbanis mother. Shumbani's mother was sympathetic. She had, in the early phase of her daughter's recovery tried to convince her that her husband was alive. Shumbani however had flown into a rage and thrown a seizure. After she recovered, Shumbani's mother had decided not to contradict her delusions. This proved to be a sound decision. Shumbani's cognitive skills had recovered completely. She became a diligent and committed teacher again. Whatever recircuiting occurred in her brain had endowed in her, an unusual and unprecedented passion for learning.

Raghu suggested that they meet with the doctor who had operated on her. The surgeon was a kind old gentleman who grasped the nuances of Raghu's predicament. Yet, he could offer no easy answers. They had a long discussion on the neurological correlates of Shumbani's clinical profile. Shumbani had lost connections to an area in her brain where a bunch of fairly recent memories was stored. Old memories were preserved. However, the part of her brain was where a set of memories of a decade had been preserved had been damaged.

The surgeon averred that this was probably good for her. Trying to re-establish these tempestuous and traumatic memories could derail her recovery. In a way she was fortunate that the memories and not just the connections were gone. People exposed to terrible experiences could develop inappropriate fear responses to innocuous stimuli. This phenomenon of Post Traumatic Stress disorder affected soldiers returning from tours of duty in active battle zones. Even civilian victims of violent criminal attacks could develop this incapacitating disorder.

Raghu pondered the situation. He had a long discussion with Shumbani's mother. Everything was on track and everyone except Raghu was happy.

Shumbani was doing well as a teacher. Her recent memory and cognitive stills were excellent. Her motivation to learn was exceptional. Raghu's sons were studious and good students. The elder of the two wanted to be a pilot and the younger one, an engineer. They were doing well in school. By trying to exert and reestablish himself as Shumbani's husband and as the father of the boys, they would all be in turmoil. He decided to accept the role bestowed upon him as Shumbani's brother. This at least would give him the opportunity to be with his family and to protect them.

13. A New Visitor:

There was a new visitor to the school. A linguistic scholar and his wife had joined the mission. The scholar, whose name was George was researching the origin and evolution of languages. He was passionate about his work. He was exceptionally interested in the study of literary Malayalam. Malayalam was a 2000 years old classical language and was one of the oldest with a written script. Early inscriptions in Malayalam, etched on palm leaves, had been preserved in the Padmanabha temple at Trivandrum.

George's wife Sophia, was an enigma. Rumor was that she worked for her government. She was tall and slim with the grace of a ballerina. The contrast between her and the professor was stark. They had separate bedrooms and their demeanor did not suggest mutual attraction or intimacy.

George's visit to Kerala aroused

interest in the academic circuit of Kottayam. Many academics wanted hear and to share his erudition. Soon, George was giving a talk at the town hall. Raghu took Shumbani and the boys to the lecture. The hall was packed with the intelligentsia of Kerala. They listened in fascination as he explained the origin and evolution of humankind. The essence of human cognitive superiority had, according to him, its roots in the evolution of language.

They listened enraptured as Professor George expounded the essence of intelligence. Intelligence has three phases. The first is the recording of memories to create a knowledge depot. The second involves manipulation of memory and of knowledge archives for informed decision making. The third is the executive phase, where decisions translate into action.

We all appreciate that a large quorum of information, especially structured education is imparted through language. This is in the first phase of information acquisition. What is less apparent is the role of language in information manipulation and in decision making. Language plays a key part in the second phase. Memory engrams in the frontal lobe of the brain and knowledge repositories in the Parietal association cortices are tethered or bound by connections routed through the Caudate nucleus. Memory engrams in the Frontal lobe are information gists stored in language form.

Frontal Lobe information abstracts allow for fast manipulation to facilitate quick decisions. Their tether to detailed knowledge depots enriches the decisions taken. Consequences and outcomes of executed decisions are stored deep in the core brain as the elixir of wisdom. After the presentation was over, Shumbani went up to George. She volunteered to guide him through the nuances of Malayalam language and to be his assistant in research.

14. Shumbani finds a Mentor:

George was very happy to have Shumbani as an associate. He had heard from other teachers of the mission school as to how dedicated and driven she was. He spoke to the school principal. Shumbani could work as his associate, in addition to her school duties.

Raghu was managing the mission's estates again. In addition to the school campus, the mission had a good 20 acres of land, much of which was wild and overgrown with assorted tropical shrubbery. There was deer on the campus and the odd fox. You could hear them at night howling at the full moon. You could also hear the cackle of chicken in their coop as the odd fox hunted an easy gourmet meal.

Raghu's days were full. From morning to evening he was in the estate. He tended fruit trees spruced up hedges and platooned plantain trees and pineapple plants. His day started early, well before the first school bell tolled at 8 AM. There was no lunch break. He would be back home by five for a snack. He spent an hour every day instructing the boys in games and sports and training their bodies and minds to cope with vagaries of the world. By seven, the Boys would be back with Shumbani who supervised their school work and home assignments. Raghu- relegated to the role of uncle would sleep in the gardener's cottage after an early dinner. He would be in bed by 8 PM.

At night, around 2 in the morning, Raghu would get out of bed. Picking up his flexible Urumi sword, he would head into the garden. The swish of his whirling blade was like the rustle of breeze through the leaves. After a two-hour work-out he would have a quick wash in the garden tap before heading back to his bed for another couple of hours of rest before he started work again. No one saw him training or suspected him of midnight forays. Raghu was focused. The forging and fusion of his body and mind in Kalarippayattu kept him serene and sane.

A tranche of coconut leaf scrolls had been found at the Padmanabha swami temple. The authorities contacted George. They solicited his help to date, analyze and interpret these archives. George took Shumbani with him. They took a train to Trivandrum. A government car picked them up from the station. Shumbani was amazed at how much Trivandrum had changed since she left. The roads were crowded now. Government cars and private vehicles jostled with bullock carts for precedence on the roads. At the palace where the scrolls were now housed, George was welcomed as a VIP. He introduced Shumbani as his research associate. Together they sat in the palace library analyzing and deciphering the script. George took photographs and Shumbani made drawings. It was evening before they rose from their chairs. They thanked the museum curate. They returned to the hotel where their rooms had been booked. Leaving their papers, overnight bag and camera in George's hotel room, Shumbani took George for a guided tour of Trivandrum.

15. An intellectual Romance:

Thiruvananthapuram, renamed Trivandrum during the British reign, gets its name from Lord Ananta, deity of the Padmanabha Swami Temple. The Padmanabha Swami temple is the richest temple in the world. The vaults of the temple contain countless treasures. Some of the vaults are believed to contain spirits who would curse anyone who would disturb their slumber. Shumbani showed him around the old town explaining history which she had experienced and grown up with. It was dark now. They returned to the hotel. Shumbani went up with George to his room. She would put all the documents they had gathered in sequence. George was tired. He changed into his pajamas and slept.

It was almost midnight when Shumbani finished her work. George was fast asleep on one side of the double bed. After a quick wash, she changed into her night clothes. Quietly, she lay down on the other side. Drawing a sheet over herself, she drifted off to sleep. George woke up sensing a weight on the bed. He looked across and found Shumbani snuggled under the bed sheets. Smiling, he slept again.

Walking down the streets of Trivandrum had stirred echoes of the past in Shumbani's brain. She woke up sweating profusely. She might have cried out in her sleep. George woke up, hearing her. He threw his arm comfortingly around. Shumbani felt secure and at peace. Both slept in reassured comfort till morning. George was up first. Moving carefully to avoid disturbing the girl, he got up and got ready. Shumbani woke up. She felt no embarrassment. Their train was at 10 am. They had breakfast in the hotel.

In the train they talked of future plans, both personnel and on language research. George had been invited by the Egyptian consul to visit and to assess a bunch of recently discovered parchments. He wanted Shumbani to go with him. His work had focused on the common origin of languages. Language had evolved as a means of communication between individuals of a tribe in Mesopotamia or maybe Africa. As tribes migrated, they carried their languages with them. Languages evolved with use.

Shumbani proposed a new paradigm. Was it possible that languages evolved within individual brains as a result of Brain development. Our brains developed a code like the code in a computer ton store information for rapid use. Language thus developed as a tool to facilitate cognition. This code was verbalized as individuals shared information. The phonetic code and later, the scrolled equivalent was a manifestation of human cognitive exuberance. Sounds and scripts were codified by interaction between individuals of the tribe and species. The primary hypothesis of Shumbani's hypothesis was that language evolved primarily as an intrinsic cognitive tool. Later, this was fine-tuned as a phonetic and later written mode of communication.

George sensed that the differences in perception of the two of them reflected a conflict between cultures. The west was evolving as an information driven civilisation. Learning was the key to everything. Hindu philosophy and Indian culture emphasized wisdom as the prime mover of human psyche. Information was necessary to produce information. Wisdom was the crux that allowed our athma to commune and collaborate in the paramathma. George decided to keep his mind open. The information from his research would enrich his search for his own soul.

They reached Kottayam and headed back to the mission. The chemistry between the two of them was obvious and intense to all. Raghu hid his inner distress. Shumbani believed he was her brother. George was a great man. With him by her side Shumbani would bloom and blossom on the world stage. His sons would have opportunities for self-actualization which they would otherwise be deprived of. He would not be selfish. He decided to teach himself to share her happiness.

Sophia seemed blithely unconcerned. Shumbani moved into a room adjacent to George's. George had an eye watering tranche of books on language which they referenced extensively. They worked late into the night. George was often the first to retire to bed. On the nights when she was scared or lonely Shumbani would snuggle in with him till the early hours of the morning.

16. Sophy and Raghu:

Raghu was convinced that Sophia was not and had never been married to George. George was her cover for her Kerala visit. He was convinced that she was on some clandestine mission. From what he had seen of George and his work, the work Sophy was doing was presumably to some laudable end. What exactly Sophy was doing remained a mystery.

Sophy spend her days exploring Kottayam town. She would leave in the morning with a lunch pack, a note book and a bottle of lime juice. It would be nearing sundown when she returned. Shumbani's mother was worried about Sophy's safety. One day she suggested that Raghu accompany Sophy on her town jaunts. He could escort her to safe zones and could tell her a bit about the history and ethos of the central keara culture.

The mission car dropped them both at the local newspaper office. Raghu was with Sophy as she met the editor. Sophy claimed to be a researcher from the United Kingdom. She was doing a project on women's education and rights in the Indian Subcontinent. Over the past one month she had visited the colleges in Kottayam and Chenganashery and interviewed teachers and students. She wanted the editor's perspective on the hope, scope and hindrances to youth education.

The editor was very candid in his appraisal. The primary scrouge which was poisoning the youth of Kerala today, was the influx of illicit drugs. He was convinced that someone was deliberately targeting the state's youth to destroy its potential. They had tea and snacks in the editor's office. Raghu was introduced as the estate manager of the mission. H her husband had come to the mission on deputation.

After they left the newspaper office they walked down to the children's library. There was a shady garden where they could sit and talk. Sophy had decided to confide in Raghu. Sipping a milk shade she told him her story. Sophy worked for British Intelligence. The flood of drugs into the west had taken ominous proportions. A whole generation was being lost to the depraved demotivating scrouge. She had been tasked to investigate the Indian Angle.

Poppy plantations were flourishing in Myanmar, in Afghanistan and in some North Western provinces of Pakistan with the tacit approval of the governments concerned. International pressure and supervision prompted the Pakistan government to crack down on export through its ports. The Drug dealers were now routing their shipments through India. Crossing the porous borders of Punjab, drugs were being distilled and purified in Indian factories. Consignments from Kerala had been found routed through

Europe to markets in the west.

Sophy showed Raghu the statistics she had collected. The incidence of habitual drug use amidst the student population in the colleges of Kerala was high. Even more alarming was the realization that the majority of users were using distilled and synthetic products. These drugs were much more potent. It was also true that their addiction liability after single use was very high.

The prime reason for the spike in drug abuse was availability. Factories producing synthetic and semisynthetic drugs needed potency tests in a captive population. By hooking a bunch of youth to drugs, these factories could tailor purity and potency through field trials.

George and Shumbani had flown to Egypt for their assignment. George planned to fly down to his house in Germany after that. He and Shumbani would finalise their magnum opus on the evolution and origin of languages. George had also suggested that they could look at shifting Shumbani's two boys to the international school in his city. Here, they could continue studies in English while developing proficiency in German.

That night when Raghu was going through his Kalari paces he had the uncanny sensation of being watched. The house was dark. Shumbanis mother and the two boys were asleep in the master bedroom. There were no lights in Sophy's room. From the corner of his eye, he glimpsed a movement on the balcony. There was an intruder on the terrace. His Children and the ladies were in danger.

He edged behind a curtain of bushes before sprinting towards the house. Vaulting over the terrace ledge he landed on the balls of his feet. There was no one on the terrace. A shadow flitted near the stairs as someone scurried down. In a trice, Raghu reached the stairs. In the darkness he could sense more than see the fleeing figure. In three steps he reached the intruder. His powerful forearm was round the victim's neck as he prepared to squeeze the captive into submission.

Abruptly his forearm eased its chokehold. The body against his sweaty rippled chest had gone limp. With shock, he realized that it was a woman. Her soft silky hair flowed over his arms as her head lolled forward. Her knees had buckled. Had he killed her?

He lifted the limp figure in his arms and moved up the stairs to the terrace. His hunch was confirmed. It was Sophy. Gently he laid her down on the terrace. The moonlight brough a gleam of gold to her pale skin. She was barely breathing. Taking in a deep breath he fastened his lips over her open mouth in an airtight seal. He blew hard inflating her chest. As he relaxed
the warm air from her chest blew its sweet aroma back into his mouth. He blew in again.

He continued breathing for her, his eyes closed in raptured commitment and silent prayer.

He continued his mouth-to-mouth resuscitation. Suddenly he felt her arms snaking around his neck. Opening his eyes, he looked at her face. Her eyes were wide open and smiling. As his mouth moved away in embarrassment, she mumbled. "You almost killed me. I need some more CPR". Her mouth fastened around his again. He felt her tongue teasing him. As he tried to get up, her long legs wrapped around his back as she wrestled him down.
Raghu could feel his throbbing emotions as he reciprocated. They were both submerged in a roaring tidal wave of passion. Afterward he held her spasming jerking body firmly against his, till her eyes opened and she kissed him again. They lay on the terrace watching the stars wink and fade away.

17. Sophy's Secret:

Later that day they went for another of Sophy's interviews. The NGO with its focus on women's welfare was aided by the United States Government. The lady in charge was eager to show them the books and statistics. He spoke of legal issues and women's rights. Taking Dowry was illegal but the practice was still prevalent. The patriarchy frowned upon higher education for women and on women taking up high profile jobs.

Sophy tried to steer the conversation around to alcoholism and drugs. The lady was suddenly wary. Kerela men had a weakness for alcohol. Toddy shops were more common than convenience of grocery stalls. When questioned about drug use amongst students, she chose to be evasive. Sophy and Raghu got the distinct impression that she was trying to conceal something.

After they got out, Raghu took Sophy to a movie. The hall was practically empty. The movie was a documentary cum commercial production. It depicted the life of a tribal girl who fell in love with a medical student. Sophy had no idea why he wanted her to see this film. Raghu explained how the movie was shot in the hills when he resided in the forest settlement. A BBC team had come to capture images of the forests of North Kerala. It was he had guided the director on the geography and the landmarks. After the landgrab, when the logging started, the film rolls had been confiscated by the government citing security concerns. Logging had been stymied by Raghu. Political power in the state had shifted. The current disposition released the documentary to the BBC. They sold the movie footage to a film maker who had woven a human-interest story into it.

After the movie, they sat in the theatre cafeteria. Raghu told Sophy his life story. He told her about himself and Shumbani. He narrated their escape from Trivandrum. He spoke of the forest settlement and of the attack by goons. Shumbani was different after the head injury. She had forgotten him and had no recollection of their life together. His children too were confused. By staking a claim on their lives he would make them relive their trauma and potentially compromise their prospects. Shumbani had developed a passion for academics and had fallen in love with George.

It was Sophy's turn. She had learned Ballet Dancing in school. A bright student, she had majored in biochemistry from Oxford. After dabbling in theatre and training in Karate, Sophy had been recruited by the British Military Intelligence department. Illicit addictive drugs were pouring into Britain, Europe and USA. Recently Military Intelligence had information that the drug influx was being directed and coordinated. Corrupting the youth was as effective in creating social chaos as any bomb. by a non-state actor. The South American Drug

Cartels, poppy planting nations and the drug factories were cogs in the wheel. Sophy was sent to India to investigate. She was tasked to track the supply route. If possible, she should also identify the factories where heroin was distilled from opium and synthetic drugs were being made. Once the routes and factories were found, international bodies could pressurize the government to act.

18.Managing a Cardamom Plantation:

Raghu and Sophy made plans. They would move to the high ranges. Sophy would need to alter her appearance a bit. She had dark hair. With a bit of skin coloring and suitable attire she could pass for a fair Malayali female. It took Sophy a week to get approvals for their plans from her head office in the United Kingdom. Military Intelligence also proffered a fair alibi.

Raghu was the new manager of a cardamom plantation in the highlands. He would reside with his wife in a traditional cottage on the estates. The cottage was built of teakwood and brick and propped up on cemented stilts. This kind of raised construct was popular with the British. These raised structures proffered protection from snakes, centipedes and scorpions.

They reached their new house in an estate

jeep. Raghu had sprouted a beard and moustache. Sophy looked very Indian, dressed in a chiffon saree and adorned with an ornate Bindi on her forehead. The previous manager had returned to England a week ago. The estate sprawled over 440 acres. A coffee estate of around 20 acres was within the premises. There was a about a hundred estate worker, most of whom came from over the border of Tamil Nadu. Harvesting season would start in September, which was a month away. Till then, they could exert a minimum degree of supervision. Raghu smiled to himself. His work would start much sooner.

They had an exotic dinner of ginger bread with venison and quail's eggs. After dinner, the supervisor left. The bedroom lights were dimmed. Raghu and Sophy sat by the window looking out over the forest.
The forest was familiar turf for Raghu. He was looking forward to his adventure. Tomorrow he would hike across the forest to the rubber factory.

Raghu sensed a soft shimmer behind him. He turned around. Sophy looked like a glimmering mermaid in her flowing chiffon kaftan. He rose to hold her. It would be a while before they were together again. They had a few hours to spend together before he left.

Raghu was ready to move by 4 in the morning. He had with him fresh water and a few provisions. Sophy had given him a camera. He would garner as much evidence as he could about the factory and then return. Sophy was crying as she bade him good bye. She had a sinister foreboding that fate had a panoply of surprises in store. She would manage the estate. The estate supervisor Rahim however made her feel uncomfortable.

19. Raghu and the Elephants:

Raghu hoisted himself out through the bed room. He landed softly on the garden floor. He was wearing sneakers and track pants with a black T shirt. The night was dark and he merged into the shadows easily. He reached the electrified fence at the estate perimeter. Vaulting over the fence he felt he was back where he belonged. Birds chattered in excitement. A python slithered down a Banyan tree root to take a better look at him. Raghu moved easily. By daybreak he was deep in the jungle. A herd of elephants milled around in the tall grass. Raghu went closer. Something had happened to cause the troop consternation.

A young elephant sensed his presence and turned round to charge. The large Matriarch put out her trunk to stop him. She had sensed Raghu's presence. Raghu was needed now. Raghu moved forward. At the matriarchs authoritative grunt, the herd pared. Raghu could now see what had happened. Two of the calves had fallen into an elephant pit. The pit had been made by illicit hunters. There were sharpened spikes at the base. The pit had been covered by tree branches and a spattering of mud. An unsuspecting elephant could step on the unsupported leafy carpet, tumble into the pit and get impaled. Two young elephant calves strayed away from the main herd and had tumbled into the pit. The calves, being small in size had not been impaled. But they were well and truly trapped.

Raghu looked around. In one corner of the pit was a tug rope. The poachers had used this during the construction of the pit. They would have left the rope to haul out the tusks after an elephant got trapped and killed. Raghu climbed down into the pit. The calves
Cluttered around him. They knew the man was there to save them. Carrying the calves out, using the rope for support was not an option. The little elephants were already too heavy. He had to figure out another way.

Raghu yanked out the spikes from the ground. Using the sharp wooden spikes, he prized away the bricks lining the pit on one side. Two of the lowermost layers of bricks were out on one side. A third layer was also removed. The elephants could not initially understand what he was doing. The Matriarch was the first to figure out the strategy. Raghu wanted the wall to crumble. She came close to the edge and started stomping the ground. It took another few hours of work before the wall collapsed. A muddy slope now led down into the pit. Guiding one of the calves to the mud slope, he tried to coax him up. The slope was too steep.

Raghu clambered out of the pit. Taking the thick tug rope, he handed over one end to the matriarch. The majestic elephant looped her trunk around the rope. Raghu tossed the rope over her shoulder and knotted it. Raghu climbed down into the pit again with the other end of the rope over his shoulder. He coaxed the larger of the two calves to the slope. He looped the rope around the little elephant's shoulder. The calf, seeing the matriarch held the rope in his trunk for a better sense of control. Raghu pushed from behind as the matriarch pulled the calf gently up the slope. He freed the calf and took the rope down to the second one. This calf was smaller and more apprehensive. Even the small elephant calf was stronger than an ox. It took all Raghu's tact and the matriarch's reassurances from above before he could be coaxed up the slope. A whoop of celebration went of the up from a tusker. Raghu was exhausted. He had not eaten anything and it was already well past sunset. He looked for his provision bag and could not find it. Where was his camera?

A gentle tap on his shoulder made him turn. He had almost forgotten the elephant herd. The young elephant stood behind. She held his camera and his provision bag in her trunk. Another elephant stood behind with a bunch or ripe plantains. They fussed around him as he ate a hearty meal. A couple of coconuts were presented to him which he de-husked. He then cracked open the shells and drank the cool water within. Coconut scrapings with sweet plantains was a delicious dessert. After the meal a gentle tusker knelt down before him. Raghu clambered up on his back. They would convey him where he wanted to go. The herd moved on towards the Tamil Nadu Border. They were a bit slow. He could have covered the ground much faster. He slept on the elephants back. He would conserve his energies for later.

It took the herd 2 days before they reached the 'rubber factory'. The factory had undergone a massive makeover. Solar panels and backup chargeable lithium batteries powered the flood lights illuminating the grounds and the security/surveillance systems. There was a generator room for powering the machinery. This diesel generator was now quiet. During the day when the factory machinery was operating, the generator would hum. There was a moat all around the premises. The herd showed him a sector where the walls had caved in and they would walk across. Raghu bid goodbye to the herd. He had planned a clandestine intelligence gathering operation. He would take photographs and make note. To arrive leading an elephant platoon was not part of his plan.

He bade the herd goodbye. The two elephant calves he rescued came to him last. The larger of the two touched his shoulder and then raised his trunk in a smart salute. The smaller one nuzzled him with a kiss on his cheek. The herd marched away. The matriarch was telling the herd. "He is one of us. This is not the first time he has saved elephant lives".

20. Raghu is Trapped.

Raghu surveyed the factory security. There was a security guard at the gate. The lights in the factory were off. If this factory were a hub of drug synthesis and purification, there should have been more security. Had Sophy been wrong in her assessment? Raghu crept up close to the factory wall. There were no windows at the ground level. He heaved himself up to a ledge on the first floor. The window above him was open. Keeping an eye on the sentry at the gate he moved in through the open window. There was a whirling sound above his head. Even before the net closed around him, Raghu realized that he was trapped.

The hunter's net was woven of reinforced Nylon. It was strong enough to hold a lion. The rope holding the net had snapped back. Raghu was bundled up inside a net. The lights of the factory came on. Two burly men in battle fatigues walked into the room. They stood- feet apart watching him. "This is the superman they sent to break up our operation. They were taunting him. The whole US army failed to do what he had been asked to do." "Shall we finish him off. Put him out of his misery?" "No- the boss is here and wants to meet him. We also have a surprise package for him, which will be coming soon". Four more storm troopers had come in. They shackled Raghu's arms and legs before getting him out of the net. They strapped him to a chair. Raghu was helpless. He would bide his time. The enemy had yet to show his hand. He wondered what the surprise package was.

His chair was near a window. Through the reinforced glass he could see a limousine drawing up. Another jeep was following at a distance. The front door had opened. The men in the room seemed nervous. The visitor was an important man. The man was sensibly dressed in brown flannel trousers and an off white, half sleeved shirt. His fair skin and orange hair had been bronzed and bleached brown in the tropical sun. Two professional looking armed bodyguards flanked him. He pulled his chair up, close to Raghu.

21. An offer spurned:

He introduced himself. "My name is William. They call me Chapo. I am an entrepreneur from Columbia." Raghu saw Sophy freeze. So this was the notorious 'El Chapo', kingpin of the international drug trade. His cruelty and menace were legendary. Interpol had placed a multi-million-dollar prize on his head. There had been no takers. "I have been keeping track of both of you. He was speaking to Sophy. "My friends in military intelligence speak highly of your skills". He turned to Raghu. "I watched you from the time you beheaded that diabolical politician. You single handedly routed a large gang of crooks and destroyed their illicit logging operation. I could use a man like you. I was hoping you would join my organization". Seeing Raghu's look of defiance, the man continued. "I have an asset with me that will help you make up your mind". Turning to his bodyguards, he barked a command, "Okay. Bring her in. Tell Rashid to wait outside".

Sophy looked disheveled. She was in a pajama suit and her hands were cuffed behind. Raghu tried to hurl himself forward with the chair. The men standing behind had anticipated the move. One of the men held the chair firmly while another slipped a nylon cable around Raghu's neck. "You are brave", William acknowledged. "She has not been hurt or molested". Raghu looked at Sophy. She nodded. It was true. "If you join my organization, no one will dare raise their eyes to her. If you refuse, I will find some other talent elsewhere. I will leave you to my men. They can do whatever they want with both of you. You have four hours to make a decision. Till then you are under my protection".

"Rashid is my man. He is a womanizer with a bad reputation. But he is efficient. He had recorded your conversation at the estate manager's house. He has his eye on Sophy. If you defy me, you will be dead and she will be his".

Raghu and Sophy were made to stand. They were no longer tied to their chairs. The handcuffs were still on. Some sophisticated guns There were 10 armed men in the room. Raghu was showing restraint. It was not yet time to breakout. The gunmen looked dispassionate and able. They would drill bullets into the two of them without compunction. Raghu and Sophy were being herded out of the hall. Outside the main door the limousine engines were purring. Rashid was in the jeep. He smirked in contempt as Raghu and Sophy were pushed and prodded out of the factory building at gun point.

William paused before getting into the limousine. He turned to the prisoners. "My private plane will fly out to Switzerland from Kochi in six hours. If you are joining me, you will be on that flight". He got into the limousine and the car moved on. In an hour the limousine would be on the highway. In three hours, William would be back at his hotel getting ready for his flight.

22. A Mammoth task:

Raghu and Sophy, both securely shackled were taken to watchman's hut by the side of the factory. They were strapped to their chairs. Rashid was in the room with them. He was looking at Sophy with unadulterated lust. Only William's assertion that he was under his protection made him leash his libido. Raghu looked away as he heard an elephant trumpet in the distance. The matriarch of the herd was calling someone. A minute later he heard another louder trumpet. This was the lone tusker, Murugan. A majestic animal, Murugan had left the herd. If the matriarch was calling him back, she would have some critical mission for him. Raghu understood the language of elephants. He had lived in their midst in his settlement days. There was a lot of trumpeting going on in the forest. Something was brewing.

Williams was working on his laptop in the backseat of the limousine as it made a steady pace through the forest road. There was a sudden screech of brakes. Williams looked up in irritation. What he saw froze his blood. Blocking the road stood a huge tusker. He seemed to be frothing at the mouth in anger. Before he could react, the tusker charged. Rearing up on his hind legs the elephant stood in front of the car. There was crunch and a crash as it tromped the car's engine. The chassis snapped in half and the roof slid off. Williams was still strapped to the seat when Murugan impaled him with his tusk. Tearing him off the seat he tossed him high into the air. Williams was dead before his body hit the ground.

There was a commotion outside the factory. A storm seemed to be blowing. Tree branches were breaking and steel girders of the building were crashing down. They could hear men scream. Rashid ran to look out of the window. "Elephants", he screamed. There was a crash as the wall of the watch man's hut crumbled to dust. As the dust cleared, they could see the outline of a large elephant. Rashid was cringing in the corner, sobbing as he tried to make himself as inconspicuous as possible. Sophy had seen the look on Raghu's face. There was no fear. She felt confident too.

The matriarch took in the scene at one glance. Charging in, she wrapped her trunk around Rashid. She hoisted the quivering man high into the air before hurling him at the factory wall. The man seemed stuck to the wall for a minute before he slid down to the ground. The elephant rolled him over. She seemed to be looking for something. She lifted the dying man into the air and shook him. A bunch of keys tumbled to the floor. Tossing the man casually over her rump and into the rubble, she gently lifted the keys in her trunk and took the keys over to Raghu. Gently she placed it in his manacled hand. It took Raghu a while to figure out the correct key and to unlock his cuffs. Once his hands were free, he could unstrap his hands and legs and then free Sophy. They both stood up gingerly.

23. The Last Post:

Raghu and Sophy looked around. It looked like a war zone. The factory walls had been demolished by the elephants. The roof, quaintly intact, rested on the ground. The elephant battalion had reassembled. The battle was over. They retreated. The matriarch trumpeted a message. From the forest, Murugan the Giant tusker trumped back. The work was done. Raghu and Sophy looked around the site of devastation. Rashid's jeep was intact. The matriarch had paused and was looking at them. Raghu retrieved Rashid's keys. He had tossed them away after he had unshackled their handcuffs. The jeep keys were there in the loop.

The matriarch watched as Raghu and Sophy walked to the jeep. The engine started smoothly. He shifted into gear. Everything seemed to be working. Sophy hopped into the passenger seat. The matriarch seemed to smile in silent satisfaction as she sashayed back to her herd. She trumpeted once. There was a return trumpet from the forest. Raghu smiled. Murugan had been appraised. They drove down the jungle road to the highway. This was the route, William had taken. The road meandered through lush green forest.

Their jeep rounded a curve and then stopped. Sophy had nodded off to sleep exhausted. Her eyes opened as Raghu applied the brakes. Sophy looked ahead in amazement. A giant tusker, stood in the middle of the road blocking their path. She felt no fear as he ambled down to the open jeep. She sat still as the magnificent animal appraised her. He touched her cheek with his trunk. Raising his trunk into the air, he let out a long joyous trumpet. The king of elephants had just appreciated and approved his daughter in law.

Murugan stepped aside and seemed to nod to Raghu. Raghu started the jeep. He drove slowly ahead as Murugan shuffled off into the forest.

24. Epilogue

The estate managers house had been spruced up to receive guests. Raghu and Sophy sat out on the balcony. Their twins were being readied by a maid for the arrival of their cousins. George and Shumbani were in India as guests of honor for International Literature Festival which was being held at Bangalore in India for the first time. Their thesis on the origin of languages had received world-wide acclaim. The unanswered question on whether the evolution of language was the cause or the effect of human cognitive exuberance fascinated both the worlds of science and literature.

George and Shumani were blessed with twins a year into their marriage. With the two sons from Shumbani's previous marriage, they had a fairly large family. The whole family was down in India for the fest. They had hired a Toyota Innova and had driven down. Sophy had arranged

Breakfast for the family. Raghu had arranged a surprise treat for them.

The Innova drew up at the porch. The family tumbled out. Raghu looked at Shumbani. She had changed. The air of cultured sophistication around her was amazing. She had about her, an aura of confidence evolved over years of teaching and academic debates. George was still the studious academic. Raghu looked at his two sons. They were strong and bright boys. Their ebullient confidence and unaffected poise reflected intelligence buffed by exceptional parenting and erudite guidance. They rushed to hug Raghu, calling him uncle. The two sets of twins soon got along like a house on fire.

Breakfast was mix of cuisines. Traditional Kerala Puttu and plantains was supplemented with quail's eggs and fried fresh water fish. After eating, they trooped out on the terrace. Raghu had promised them a short tour of the forest. George was a little concerned about snakes. The twins were small and walking them through dense tropical forest did not seem prudent.

From the terrace Raghu gave a long low whistle. There was trumpet from the forest. As they watched, a troop of elephants paraded into the garden. Raghu helped the families mount their magnificent steeds. They trooped into the forest. As the majestic procession passed through the jungle, animals and birds of all hues lined up to see and be seen. Sophy and her family clicked away with their cameras. It was early evening before they returned to the bungalow. George opted for an early supper. They all decided to join him. Early next morning they would be driving to Kochi for a flight to Paris.